This Little Tiger book belongs to:

_____

_____

_____

For granny bears everywhere
~ A R

For Rosie, a most lovely grandma!
~ A E

LITTLE TIGER PRESS LTD,
an imprint of the Little Tiger Group
1 Coda Studios,
189 Munster Road, London SW6 6AW
www.littletiger.co.uk
First published in Great Britain 2018
This edition published 2019
Text copyright © Alison Ritchie 2018
Illustrations copyright © Alison Edgson 2018

Alison Ritchie and Alison Edgson have asserted
their rights to be identified as the author and illustrator of this
work under the Copyright, Designs and Patents Act, 1988

A CIP catalogue record for this book is available from the British Library
All rights reserved • ISBN 978-1-84869-836-9
Printed in China • LTP/1800/3382/0820
2 4 6 8 10 9 7 5 3

Me and My Grandma

Alison Ritchie • Alison Edgson

LITTLE TIGER
LONDON

Me and my grandma
are ready to play.
We go on adventures
and stay out all day!

We race through the woods
to our favourite tree
And scramble up high –
there's a whole world to see!

We splash in the puddles,
one after the other.
If the water's too deep,
I have to take cover!

Gran cartwheels downhill,
she's not scared at ALL.
I roll like a hedgehog
curled up in a ball.

We find special pebbles
to skim in the stream.
They bounce – *plip, plip, plop*.
We make such a good team!

If I tumble and fall,
Grandma squeezes me tight.
A bear-hug from her
can make everything right.

We lie on the grass
and look up at the sky
To spot funny shapes
in the clouds floating by.

If the weather is sunny,
we go for a swim.
Gran dives like an ace
and I belly-flop in!

When we get hungry,
we catch our own tea.
A big fish for Gran
and a tiddler for me.

As we set off for home
in the soft evening light,
I count sleepy birds
tucked in safe for the night.

My gran makes up stories
(and I join in too!)
About a small bear
and a grandma – guess who?

Me and my gran
have the BEST time together.
I wish our adventures
could go on for EVER!